**The Shark-Man
of Kapu Bay**

LOOK FOR OTHER HAWAI'I CHILLERS:

#2
The Curse of Pele

#3
***The Missionary's
Ghost***

The Shark-Man
of Kapu Bay

P.J. Neri

3565 Harding Avenue Honolulu, Hawai'i 96816

Printed in the United States of America

Cover design by Carol Colbath
Moon logo by Kevin Hand

Library of Congress Cataloging-in-Publication Data

Neri, P.J.
        The shark-man of Kapu Bay / P.J. Neri.
            p.   cm.   (Hawai'i chillers ; 1)
        Summary: Alika and his sister Jamie find out
the truth about the ancient Hawaiian Shark-Man.
        Includes glossary.
        ISBN 1-57306-030-5
        1. Hawaii – Juvenile fiction. 2. Sharks – Hawaii –
Juvenile fiction. 3. Horror tales. [1. Hawaii – Fiction.
2. Sharks – Hawaii – Fiction. 3. Horror stories]
I. Title.   II. Series.
PZ7.N471Sha 1997   [Fic]–dc20

CHAPTER ONE

"Uncle Paka! Over here!"

Me and Jamie ran to meet our uncle as he got off the plane.

"Howzit, you guys," he said, laughing as he hugged us both.

Hanging on to his arms, we tugged him across the Hawaiian Air lounge to where Mom was waiting.

"Hi, there, little sister," he told her.

"*Aloha nui loa*, Paka! Welcome home," Mom said. Smiling, she draped the *pīkake* leis she and my sister had made around his neck. Then she kissed his cheek.

"Did you have a good flight?"

"The best."

"That's great. We're really glad you're back. Alika and Jamie can't wait to spend some time with you. You're still their favorite uncle. Right, kids?"

"Right!" we both said at the same time.

He laughed. "I'm looking forward to it, too. Are you sure you have enough room at your place, Lani?" Paka asked, pushing his straight black hair out of his eyes. "I can rent a room in town, if it's too much trouble."

Uncle Paka and Kawika, our step-dad, had never met. I guess Paka thought Mom's new husband might not want him to stay with us.

"Rent a room? No way! You're family. Besides, Kawika can't wait to meet you. Really, it's no trouble at all."

"Thanks, Lani."

She laughed. "Don't be too grateful."

"Why not?" Uncle Paka asked.

"Because you're sharing Alika's room." Mom smiled. "Is that okay?"

"It's fine with me." Uncle Paka grinned at me. "Okay with you, big guy?"

"It was my idea," I told him. "You get the bed by the window. I get the wall."

"Sounds great," he said, and gave me a high five.

I couldn't stop smiling as we waited for Uncle Paka's bags at the baggage carousel. Neither could Jamie.

We hadn't seen Uncle Paka for two years, and we'd really missed him. I knew Mom was happy, too, because she couldn't stop smiling, either.

She looked so pretty in her blue *mu'umu'u*, with frilly white orchids in her hair.

My sister, Jamie, is a year younger than me. She looks a lot like Mom. They're both kind of short, with small features, curly dark-brown hair and big eyes. The only difference is, Mom always wears her hair up, while Jams's hair hangs down her back. It's untidy, most of the time, but she gets mad when I say that.

Paka called Mom a month ago to tell her that the Hawaiian Archaeological Association had asked him to work on a special project in the islands.

Mom had asked him to stay with us while he was here.

Uncle Paka's a famous archaeologist. From when we were small kids, he's sent me and Jamie postcards and neat things from all over the world. This would be his first project in Hawai'i, though. Until now, his "digs" had been in places like the Valley of the Pharaohs in Egypt or in prehistoric caves in France.

Everyone says me and Paka look alike. I guess we do. We're both tall and kind of skinny. We both have straight dark hair and brown eyes, too. The only difference is, I don't wear glasses, and Uncle Paka does. He can't see anything without them. Neither can Mom, but she wears contacts.

As we drove out of the airport, she asked Paka about the project he'd be working on.

"Sorry, you guys. I'm not allowed to talk about the project yet," he told us as we whizzed along the freeway toward the North Shore. "All I can tell you is that it's about something another archaeologist found in Kāmalū Valley."

"Kāmalū Valley?" My ears pricked up.

"Right. It's not far from where you're living."

He was right about that. The valley was very close to where we lived at Puakea on the North Shore of O'ahu. In fact, it was me and Jamie's favorite place to play.

There were no houses in "our" secret valley. No construction, cars, trash or crime. There were only trees, flowers, rocks, water—and us kids. I'd never seen a bird, a wild pig or a mongoose there.

"What did he find?" I asked, curious. "Artifacts? Bones? Ancient Hawaiian burial caves?"

"Unh uh. Nothing like that. Just some drawings. On rocks."

"You mean petroglyphs?"

I was surprised. We played there all the time, so we knew every inch of the place. But I'd never seen any petroglyphs.

My uncle nodded. "That's right, Einstein. Petroglyphs."

I held up the lucky rock I wore on a cord around my neck. "Stuff like this, you mean?"

"Where did you find that?" Uncle Paka demanded.

His eyes blazed as the black stone swung slowly to and fro.

He reached for it with a huge hand.

"Give that to me, Alika. Right *now!*"

CHAPTER TWO

I jerked away before he could grab the cord from my neck.

"No way! It's mine! My lucky rock."

Was Uncle Paka kidding around, or what?

No. It was no joke, I decided. His eyes had really scared me. I'd never seen him look like that.

"You're wrong about that, Alika," Uncle Paka said. His narrow face was still stern. His brown eyes were serious behind his thick glasses. "According to my research, that petroglyph is probably *bad* luck, not good. It might even be dangerous. Please, take it off. I don't want you getting hurt, big guy."

"What's so special about an old rock, anyway?" Jamie piped up from the seat next to me. "How could such a small little thing be dangerous?"

"I can't tell you yet, honey," Uncle Paka said, turning to look at her. "You just have to trust me."

I snorted. "Yeah, right."

"Alika, I'm sorry I yelled at you," he began, turning to me. "But seeing that—that *thing* around your neck! Well, it really scared me." He made a face.

"Maybe you should take it off, hmm, honey?" Mom frowned as she looked at me in the rearview mirror. "Until Uncle says you can wear it again."

"But it's not dangerous, Mom. Honest! It keeps me safe. Like a lucky charm." I crossed my arms over my chest and scowled.

I was so mad, I couldn't look at Uncle Paka.

He'd been back less than two hours, but already he was making trouble for me.

For a second, I wished he'd stayed in Egypt or France, or wherever he'd been.

"Alika's right. The rock's lucky. It saved him from the shark," Jamie explained.

"What shark?" Mom asked. She looked at me in the mirror again. "Alika? What shark?"

Oh, *man!*

"Jamie. Shut up," I hissed.

She was only trying to be helpful. I knew that. But I'd warned her not to say anything about the shark in front of Mom. She was just making things worse for me.

"Alika. I asked you a question," Mom said again. "What shark?"

"It's just a game we play, Mom," I lied. "When we're swimming in-the bay. The other guys are the surfers. Me and Randy take turns at being the shark. It's a cool game. Like tag. Right, Jamie?"

"Right. It's called Sharks and Surfers. Alika's real good at it," Jamie said. "He always gets away from Randy." She flashed me a smile.

I didn't like lying to Mom, but she would never let us go swimming again if she found out what happened last August.

It had been the week before school started.

Me, Jamie and some friends from our street had gone swimming and diving in Kāmalū Bay, right below the valley.

By late afternoon, the others were tired. Randy, Travis, Kuʻulei and Junior went home. Me and Jamie decided to stay a little bit longer.

I was diving several yards off shore. Jamie was collecting shells on the sand.

As I made my last dive, I felt something rough bump my back. It stung so bad, I swallowed water. Still coughing, I surfaced to look around. Had a surfer or a surfboard banged into me?

I wish.

Cutting through the water was the black dorsal fin of a huge shark. It was headed straight for me! Its jaws were wide open, ready to attack.

I swam for my life!

My heart was pounding as I raced for the beach.

Sharks have bad eyesight. They attack people because humans look like seals in the water.

Sharks *eat* seals.

If I didn't outswim it, I'd be *sashimi* for a shark!

On the sand, Jamie was screaming. "HURRY! HURRY! IT'S COMING! OOOH, IT'S COMING! FASTER, GO FASTER!"

She jumped up and down as I staggered up the beach.

"Alika, oh, thank goodness! You made it! Oh, I was so scared!" she sobbed.

With a groan, I dropped to the sand.

My back burned as my chest pumped in and out.

I was so tired, so sore, I couldn't catch my breath.

Like a beached whale, I lay on my back and closed my eyes.

I couldn't forget the shark's toothy grin. The

way its jaws had opened, wider and wider. Those rows of jagged teeth!

"Oh, nooo. You're bleeding," Jamie whispered. "The shark got you!"

Her face was chalky under its tan. Her huge brown eyes were frightened. Hands shaking, she pressed a clean towel to my back.

I looked over my shoulder.

It wasn't a bite. The shark's rough skin had left a huge graze down my back. Blood was oozing from it, onto Jams's pink towel.

"Don't cry, okay? It's no big t'ing. We'll tell Mom I fell off my bike, okay? I'll be fine, honest."

"You promise, 'Lika?"

She hadn't called me 'Lika since she was in kindergarten.

"Yeah. I promise."

She blinked the tears away. "You almost got killed. That shark tried to attack you. Then it turned away. Look! It's still out there."

Jamie was right. I could see its dark fin, circling around and around.

It's waiting, I thought. *Waiting for me.*

I don't know why I believed that, but I did.

I sat on the sand and shivered as I tried to catch my breath. It was a while before I realized there was something in my hand. I was holding it so tightly, my fingers were white.

I opened my fist. Lying on my palm was a shiny black stone.

It was the size and shape of a shark's tooth, with a hole in one end for a string.

On one side was the drawing of a strange creature. It had a shark's head and a toothy upside-down shark grin. But its body, arms and legs were human.

Sort of.

Jamie often teased me about it, but I'd worn my lucky stone ever since that day. I was convinced that somehow it had saved my life.

I told myself I'd never take it off. Not for bed. Not for the shower.

Not even for my favorite uncle.

It protected its owner from sharks.

Uncle Paka took all of us to eat at Zippy's on the way home. Mom called Kawika at his working place and he met us there.

I ordered the steak, cooked rare, although I knew it grossed Jams out. I smothered my fries with gallons of ketchup. It looked just like blood.

By the time we got to dessert—banana splits and brownie delights—I wasn't mad at Jams or my uncle anymore.

I was too full to be mad at anyone.

I fell asleep that night while Uncle Paka was talking about his dig in the Valley of the Pharaohs.

That's probably why I had the dream.

In it, me and Uncle Paka were exploring a pyramid. I was excited as we walked down sandy stone steps. We were going to open a burial chamber that had been closed for thousands of years!

At the bottom of the steps, Uncle Paka turned a secret lever in the wall. It looked like the tail of a stone crocodile.

The hinges groaned like someone being tortured. Then a hidden door swung open.

We twisted and turned through several musty outer chambers to reach the central burial chamber.

In the middle was the mummy case, with strange carvings on the outside. Uncle Paka said the carvings were a picture of the person inside.

I couldn't believe my eyes. The figure on the lid looked like the shark-man on my lucky rock!

It was so weird.

"Look at all the stuff in here! It's like a

museum," I said, looking around.

"The Egyptians believed in reincarnation. That means being born, living and dying over and over again.

"They thought their king would need all these things in his next life," Uncle Paka explained. "So they buried them with him."

Beautiful vases, plates of food, clothes, chariots and weapons were stacked around the chamber. Some of the things looked like solid gold.

"This is the sarcophagus of the Shark God," my uncle told me. His eyes glowed strangely. "You must open it, boy!"

"Me? Unh uh. NO WAY!" The Egyptian king had been dead for thousands of years. Like, I really wanted to look inside his burial casket.

Yeah. Right!

"Alika! Look at me!"

I gazed into Uncle Paka's eyes. Some choice! I couldn't look away, no matter how hard I tried.

"You must open it, Alika," he murmured softly. "You alone possess the secret power. You have been chosen by the gods. Open it. *Now.*"

It had something to do with Uncle Paka's eyes and the way they glowed. I didn't want to do it. But I reached for the heavy lid, anyway.

I just couldn't help myself.

"I-have-been-chosen," I repeated like a robot. "I-alone-possess-the-secret-power."

Slowly, I lifted the heavy lid—and screamed.

CHAPTER THREE

There was a mummy inside, wrapped in moldy brown bandages. It smelled stink, like rotten fish.

But that wasn't why I screamed. I screamed because the mummy was *moving!* As I raised the lid, it sat up and unwound its bandages.

Beneath them was a shark-man, just like the one on my lucky rock. It had dead shark eyes and a jagged, toothy grin. The rest of its body was human, with dark-gray skin and arms and legs that looked normal.

"RAAARRGGH!" it roared. "RAAAR-RGGH"

Still roaring, it sprang at me.

I felt its razor teeth scrape my back and howled in terror.

I was going to be *poke* for the shark-man!

Blood spurted over my fingers like ketchup over french fries as I bolted through the pyramid.

"Come back! You have been chosen, boy!" it roared, chasing after me. "RAARRGGH! RAARRGGH!"

I slammed into walls and stuff in my terror to

escape the monster.

Twisting and turning, I raced through the pyramid. I ran until my lungs were bursting. Up steep stone stairs. Down long, narrow passages. Around sharp corners.

I ran until I couldn't run anymore. Until there was nowhere left to go.

I'd reached a dead end.

There was a solid stone wall behind me. No doors or windows. No stairs. There was only one way out.

Back the way I'd come.

And the shark-god was coming that way!

I could hear it snuffling as it dragged itself closer. Its huge, swaying shadow filled the pyramid wall. The shadow's jaws opened, wider and wider.

I pressed myself back against the icy stone. I tried to melt into it. To shrink. To vanish.

My heart was pounding so hard, I could hear it thundering in my ears.

Cold sweat trickled down my spine. More rolled off my forehead.

One snap, a single gulp, and I'd be gone. Just like that.

Aloha 'oe, Alika Kekoa.

I would never go to college, like Mom wanted. I'd never be a marine biologist or a forest ranger, either. I would never learn to play guitar. I would never go to the beach again with Ku'ulei Foster.

"NOOO! Dad! Daaad! It's gonna eat me!" I screamed. "Daaad! Help meeee! Help meeee. NOOO!"

"Alika. Alika, wake up!"

"Dad? Is that you?"

"No, big guy. It's me. Uncle Paka."

"Don't make me open it! *Please.*"

"Hey, you're okay. It was just a dream."

Heart pounding, I opened my eyes.

Uncle Paka was sitting on my bed. In the moonlight from the open window, I could see his face.

His eyes weren't glowing. They weren't dead shark-eyes, either. They just looked worried.

Worried about me.

"It was just a dream," I murmured. "Just a dumb, stupid dream."

"Too much steak and ice cream, huh?" he whispered.

Everyone else in the house was asleep. The room was dark.

"I guess so." I leaned up on one elbow. He squeezed my shoulder.

I didn't say anything, but I was really glad he was there.

"Uncle? Can me and Jams come with you tomorrow?"

"To the valley, you mean?"

"Yeah."

"Sure. But what about school?" he whispered.

"There's no school tomorrow. It's Saturday."

"That's right. Must be jet lag. I forgot. Sure, you can come. Better yet, I have some work you two can do for me. I'll pay you."

"Minimum wage?" We'd been talking about wages and stuff at school. I knew my rights.

"Hey. At least." He laughed.

I grinned. "Sure. We'll be there."

He nodded and stood up. "Get some sleep for now, big guy." He squeezed my shoulder. "We leave at seven, sharp. Ready or not."

I'd never noticed how gloomy and silent the valley was until the next morning. Or how still.

I guess that was how it got its name. Kāmalū Valley means the Peaceful Valley, I think.

Red cardinals were singing in the mango tree when we left our house. On the lawn, mynas and sparrows were squabbling over the bread-crumbs Mom had scattered for them.

There were no birds here, though. Not so much as a single twitter or chirp.

"Is it always this quiet?" Paka asked, frown-ing.

I nodded. "Always. Except for when me and the guys are here. Then we make big noise!" I grinned.

"The guys?"

"Randy and Kuʻulei dem. The kids down our street. They're our friends."

"And what's up in that *koa* tree?" he asked. Looking up, he shaded his eyes against the sun. "A tree house?"

I nodded. "It's supposed to look like a grass shack."

"It does. That's pretty neat."

He didn't ask if he could see inside. That's what I liked about Uncle Paka.

He knew I couldn't take him up there. The others had to say it was okay first, and they weren't there to ask.

Two years ago, when Jamie was ten and I was eleven, we'd all helped to build the clubhouse.

We'd raided our dads' tool chests and carports for wood, nails, saws or hammers. Now, it belonged to all of us.

We spent every vacation in "our" valley. We climbed the trees, swung on the vines and swam in the freshwater pool below the falls.

Our summers were great! They seemed to last forever.

"Who's that?" I asked.

An older man wearing a camouflage shirt, ragged denim shorts and hiking boots was coming down the narrow trail, toward us.

Except for Uncle Paka, he was the first grown-up I'd ever seen in the valley.

When he saw us, he waved. Uncle Paka looked surprised, but he waved back.

"That's Don Honu, another local archaeologist. I wasn't expecting him. Hey, Don. Where were you when the H.A.A. tracked you down?"

"The Big Island," Don said with a grin.

When he turned his head, I saw he had a long gray ponytail. "You?"

"Cairo. I heard you were on sick leave. How are you?"

"Great. Just great. Hey, kids. Howzit?"

"These aren't just kids, Don," Uncle Paka said seriously. "I'd like you to meet my nephew, Alika, and my niece, Jamie. We call her Jams. These two are experts on the valley. They know every inch of the place. Right, guys?"

"Pretty much," I agreed modestly.

"Just about," Jams added.

"They're on the payroll as guides."

"Guides, huh? That's great. You two can save us days of work," Don said. "Here. Take a look at this."

Crouching down, he unfolded a large square of paper.

It was a map of the valley and the surrounding area.

I could see the falls, the pool and the bay where the shark bumped me. Me and my friends had called it Kapu Bay—Forbidden Bay—ever since then.

"Have you kids seen the ruins of a *heiau* anywhere around here?" Don asked.

A *heiau* is an ancient Hawaiian temple. They were built to honor the old Hawaiian gods, my grandma told me. Sacrifices were made there, too. Sometimes rocks, sometimes fish or fruits—sometimes humans.

"There's Pu'u o Mahuka above the next valley," I told Don. "They say two men from Captain Cook's crew were sacrificed there, way back."

"No, not that one. Everyone knows about that one. This one is even older. It's a—er—a fishing *heiau*, I think," Paka explained. "We're looking for broken-down walls. Rocks scattered about. Vines and grass growing over stones. The temple's probably only rubble by now. "

"There's a place like that above the falls," Jams said shyly. "It's spooky though. I don't like to go up there alone." She shivered.

"On the cliffs above the falls?" Don asked.

Paka looked excited. "Can you see the bay from up there?"

"Sure. It's got the best view in the valley," I told him.

Paka smiled. "Well, done, Jamie. I bet that's where it is."

"Before we get started, will you show Don

your lucky stone, Alika?" Paka asked me.

"Sure." He could look at it. But I wouldn't let him take it. There was something about him I didn't like.

"Where'd you find that? Here, in the valley?" Don asked, after he'd stared at it for a long, long time.

I shook my head. "When I was diving in Kapu Bay."

"Forbidden Bay?"

"I meant Kāmalū Bay."

"Was that before you had that run-in with the shark?" Paka asked. "Or after?"

He acted as if my answer didn't matter, but he'd remembered what Jamie said yesterday. That meant it *was* important.

I laughed. "You don't have run-ins with sharks, Uncle Paka."

"Alika's right," Don cut in. "One run-in, and you're *make*. Dead!"

Except for me, of course.

What he'd said started me thinking. I had a run-in with a ten-foot, man-eating shark. But I was still here.

I had a scar where the *mano's* shagreen, or rough skin, grazed my back, but that was all.

Why? I wondered. Why had the shark turned away?

Why wasn't I *make*, too?

CHAPTER FOUR

Jams was right about the fishing *heiau*.

Don and Uncle Paka found the ruins above the falls. They were up on the cliffs, right where Jams said.

The low walls had fallen down over the years, but the rocks were still there. Some were overgrown with grass, ferns or weeds. Others were buried under years of dirt.

Jams was right about it being a spooky place, too.

The hairs on the back of my neck prickled as we worked.

I kept looking over my shoulder, expecting someone to be watching me. I didn't know who, exactly.

Or *what*.

But there were only shadows. *Lots* of shadows.

For some reason, the light wasn't as bright up there. The sun didn't seem as warm.

Still, once I started work, I forgot about the gloom and the cold feeling. I was too busy following Uncle Paka's instructions to worry about that.

First, me and Jams had to find as many of the missing rocks as we could. But we weren't supposed to move them. We just had to remember exactly where they were, then show Uncle Paka or Don.

They recorded each rock in their notebooks, then gave it a number on the map grid.

We helped my uncle and his assistant all morning. Both of us worked so hard, the time just flew by.

I pretended I was Indiana Jones, finding the Temple of Doom. Jams calculated how much money we could make in a month of weekends. Then we talked about what we'd spend it on.

Jams wanted to buy Rollerblades. I wanted a Nintendo 64.

Just when we were too tired to look anymore, Uncle Paka said it was time for lunch.

Jams broke out the bentos Mom had packed for us.

Each plate had Spam, teriyaki, fried chicken, *mahimahi*, and two scoops rice. There was kim chee and takuan on the side, too. Good grinds.

We offered to share with Don.

"Thanks, guys, but I brought my lunch. It's in the car. I'll be back in a while."

Everything tasted so *'ono*, we chowed down while he was gone. It was as if we were starving!

While we ate, Uncle Paka sketched a plan of the *heiau* walls.

Afterward, he numbered the place where each rock had been found. These numbers matched the numbers we'd assigned the rocks on the grid.

When I was *pau*, I carried my piece of fried chicken to the edge of the cliff.

The meat was still bloody inside, just the way I liked it.

I ate looking down over Kāmalū Falls.

They were beautiful, like an endless silver ribbon.

Directly below them, water foamed and churned from the force of the waterfall. Big mossy boulders lined the banks.

The rest of the pool was as still as a mirror. It was deep, but so clear I could see all the way to the bottom.

Nothing.

When I finished my chicken, I held my arm out. I counted backward from three, then let go of the bone.

"Bombs away!" I muttered.

It took a while to fall, then hit the water with hardly a splash.

"Awesome shot, Indiana. A direct hit!" I told myself.

But instead of ripples, I saw a big, black shadow flash through the water. It streaked across the pool, toward the chicken bone.

Then—as if something had yanked it under the surface—the bobbing bone suddenly vanished.

So did the huge black shadow.

I blinked.

Just a second before, the pool had been empty. The water had been calm and still.

So what had cast that enormous shadow?

I shivered. An uneasy feeling stirred in my stomach.

What had grabbed that chicken bone?

Nothing I could think of, unless . . .

A dog.

I told myself it had to be a dog. It had jumped into the water after the bone. It was the only explanation.

A huge black poi dog was lost in our valley.

No big t'ing, right?

"Stay away from the edge, big guy," Uncle Paka warned. "I don't want your Mom chewing me out if you fall."

I jumped. "What? Oh, yeah. I will," I murmured.

His voice had startled me. I kept on staring at the pool way below.

Maybe I'd get another glimpse of that shadow.

"What's down there?" my uncle asked. He came to stand beside me just as Don came back.

"Huh? Oh. Nothing. I—er—I thought I saw a dog. A big one. It was swimming in the pool."

"Smart dog! Hey, how about we all go swimming this afternoon? Don? Jams? It's pretty hot for November."

"Let's see how much time we have, Paka," Don said. "We should get the *heiau* documented before dark. Now that the weeds have been cut away, a storm could wash the rocks away."

"Don's right. It's the rainy season. Sorry, kids. No swimming today."

"Some other time," I told Uncle Paka.

Secretly, I was relieved.

I wasn't ready to go swimming in the pool.

Not until I was sure about that dog.

Or whatever it had been.

It was dusk when we stopped for the day. The fading light made the pool look like blood.

Warm, fresh blood.

I shivered with pleasure.

We'd worked really hard. I was so tired, I couldn't keep up as we walked down the valley to the cars.

Don's rented Jeep Cherokee was parked beside Mom's station wagon. While Don, Uncle Paka and Jams loaded the stuff, I went into the bushes to pee.

When I came back out, both cars were gone.

Those creeps. They'd left without me.

It had grown darker, too.

Much darker.

So dark and so quiet, I could hear myself thinking.

Almost.

I swallowed.

The valley had always been my favorite place. But with the light fading, it was spooky there alone.

The trees and bushes made weird lumpy shadows that hid spooky things. The chill breeze that whispered through the leaves gave me chicken skin. The long grass rustled.

Something wasn't right. I could feel it. The valley had changed somehow. It had always been peaceful, but it wasn't peaceful anymore. It was . . . evil.

Who—or what—had changed it?

Or had I changed, instead?

I shivered. I'd better get out of there, before I found out!

I'd gone only three or four steps when a hand grabbed my ankle and pulled . . .

Chapter Five

"Lemme goooo!" I yelled, falling flat on my face in the mud and wet leaves.

But whatever it was wouldn't let go of my foot!

Panicking, I twisted around and sat up. Grunting and groaning, I tried desperately to wrench my foot free.

Then I saw the terrible monster that had snagged my ankle.

It was a man-killing root. A deadly vine.

Duh!

As I untangled the plant from around my foot, I felt so dumb.

The moment it got a little bit dark, I started freaking out, imagining things. Like a great big baby.

I could almost hear my friends.

"Nani nani boo boo!"

Mad at myself, I stood and brushed off my dirty face and knees.

I was about to head on home when an unearthly moan floated out of the shadows.

It was followed by another, then another.

"WAAWHOOOO! WAAWHOOOO!"

They were eerie, hollow sounds.

Still kneeling in the muddy grass, I froze. I could feel the hairs on the back of my neck crawling, as if I had ukus.

What had made those sounds, I wondered, my teeth chattering? Had it been ghosts? Owls? The Night Marchers? What?

"WAAWHOOOO! WAAWHOOOO!"

There it was again.

I held my breath and listened—then snorted with laughter.

The long, sad sounds weren't moaning and groaning at all. They were the sounds of a conch shell. Like at elementary school, when the May Day court marches onto the field.

The sounds had come from the falls, way at the other end of the valley.

I frowned. Who'd be blowing a conch shell here, at this time of night?

Should I ditch, or investigate?

Ditch! Run for your life! Who cares who did it? I told myself. It's better to be a live coward than a dead hero.

While I was trying to decide, I glanced across the road. It was already dark at the foot of the valley. But over by the beach, it was still light enough to see.

As I watched, I saw a dark shape rise from the ocean.

It glided up the beach, then drifted across the road toward me.

Like a gray ghost, it flitted between the shadows. Then it headed silently up the valley, toward the falls.

As it passed me, its fishy smell made me gag.

I rubbed my eyes, but I still couldn't see it clearly in the gloomy light.

Who was it, I wondered? Who'd blown the conch shell to call the diver from the water? Had an evening swim club started meeting in Kāmalū Valley? Was that it?

"Alika? Alika! Come on. Get in!"

I turned and saw Jams. She was laughing as she hung out of the car window.

Uncle Paka grinned and gunned the wagon's engine.

"Hop in, big guy. We didn't mean to leave you behind. We thought you went in Don's car."

"And Don thought you were with us," Jams explained. "That's why we drove off without you."

"It's no big deal." I scowled at them. "I know my way home."

"You weren't scared? Really? But, it's almost dark," Jams said. Her eyes were big and round.

She was afraid of the dark.

Tonight, so was I. But I wouldn't let her see it.

As I climbed into the back seat, I crossed my arms over my chest. "Duh. Do I look scared?" I asked, acting cocky.

Jams flipped her long hair over her shoulder. She propped her chin on the seat and stared at me.

"Yeah," she said after a while. "You do."

When we got home, I told Jams about the shadowy figure that had walked up from the ocean, into the valley.

"We should do something, Alika," she said. "We can't let strangers change our valley."

She was right. I had to do something.

Jams went down the street to Kuʻulei and

Junior Foster's house when we got home. I went over to the Higas'. Travis and Randy were fixing their bikes in the carport. We were all in the same grade at Puakea Intermediate School.

"You're calling a special club meeting? What about?" Randy asked when he heard.

"You'll find out tomorrow. Can you and Travis make it?" I asked. "It's important."

Randy shook his head. "Uh uh. We have church in the morning."

"Tomorrow afternoon, then. Two o'clock. At the tree house. Be there."

He nodded. "We'll be there."

All the members of the club were present and accounted for the next afternoon.

Ku'ulei and her brother, Junior Foster, arrived first, then the Higa brothers. Me and Jams were waiting for them, in the tree house.

From one window, we could see to the ocean. It was bright blue and sparkling with whitecaps that afternoon.

On the other three sides, we could see leaves and a short distance up or down the valley in each direction.

When everyone had settled down, Jams passed around a bag of chips and paper cups of juice. The guys munched while I told them what I'd seen.

"Someone was in our valley?" Ku'ulei asked. "After dark?"

I nodded.

"But why would a swim club be meeting up here at night?" Randy said. "It doesn't make sense."

"That's what I want to find out," I said, taking a handful of chips. They were shrimp. My favorite.

"Are you sure it was a real person?" Junior asked hopefully, licking his fingers. He helped himself to another handful of chips.

"Of course he is, stupid," Ku'ulei told her younger brother. She looked at me and rolled her eyes. "Right, Alika?"

I hesitated. "I guess so."

"You guess so?"

"Well, the sun *was* shining in my eyes."

"There! You see?" Junior said. "It was

probably an alien."

His brown eyes shone behind his thick lenses. His chubby face wore a big, excited smile.

"First, they take over the valley," he added. "Then, the world!"

"There are no such things as aliens," Ku'ulei insisted. She gave him stink-eye.

"Are too!"

"Are not!"

"Grow up, you two," I yelled. "This is serious."

"Yeah, Junior," Ku'ulei said cockily. "Cut it out. Tell us what you want us to do, Alika."

"We need to find out what that guy was doing in our valley. I say we take turns."

"Turns at what?"

"Watching him," Jams explained. "To find out what he's doing."

"When?"

"Alika saw him yesterday, so I say we start one week from last night."

"Saturday night? But, what about our parents?" Travis asked. He frowned. "You know our mom and dad. They'll never let us spend the night in the valley."

"Don't tell them, then. Say we're having a sleepover at our house." Ku'ulei suggested.

"And we'll tell our parents we're staying with Alika and Jams." She shot us a grin.

"All right. Let's do it," Travis agreed. He grinned back.

"Next Saturday, then. Okay with you guys?" I stuck out my hand.

The others put their hands on top of mine.

"Okay!" we all said together, and shook hands.

CHAPTER SIX

We finished work early the following Saturday. It was a hot, sticky day for November. The air was so heavy and still, I knew a tropical storm was headed our way.

The others were sweaty and covered with mosquito bites by the time we packed up our gear.

Uncle Paka said we should go swimming before we went home.

"Come on, you guys!" he yelled. He scrambled down the cliffs to the pool below.

Laughing, we followed him.

At the bottom, he peeled off his tank top. Then he carefully placed his glasses on a rock. "Last one in is a cockroach!"

"Wait," I warned him. "Don't go in there!"

"Why not? What's wrong?" Jams asked.

"Look. Over there."

White feathers were heaped on a flat rock at the side of the pool. They were covered with red stains.

It looked like paint, but it was blood. I could smell it.

"The feathers?" Uncle Paka said after he'd replaced his glasses on his nose. He was as blind as a bat without them. "What about them?"

"We haven't seen a single bird in the valley, uncle. Not *one*. Ever." I swallowed. "Maybe the animal that left the cowbird feathers ate them all?"

"Ate all the birds, you mean?"

I nodded.

Paka shook his head. "No way, Alika. That's impossible. There are no animals in the islands that are big enough to do that. You've been reading too many horror stories. It was probably just a cat."

I scowled at him. "A cat! Cats don't eat cowbirds, Uncle."

He frowned. "I guess not. But it could have been that black dog you saw, don't you think. Don? Could a dog have done that?"

Don was staring at me with a half-smile on his face.

Or was he really staring at the stone hanging around my neck?

He shrugged. "Who says it was an animal at all? Maybe it was a hunter. There are wild pigs in the valley."

"There are?" I'd never seen any.

"I bet if we looked around, we'd find the ashes of a campfire someplace. Maybe some chicken bones, too." He winked at me, as if we shared a secret. "See you on Monday!"

I gave him stink-eye and scuffed my slipper in the grit. He didn't look back as he walked away.

"Don's right. Come on, you guys. Forget about the feathers. Let's swim!" Uncle Paka said.

With a Tarzan yell, he dive-bombed into the pool.

His huge splash soaked me and Jams.

"You wait, Uncle Paka!" Jams threatened, shaking her head. Water flew around her in big fat drops. "This is war!" She pulled off her tee-shirt and shorts. Under them, she wore a bright sunflower-yellow swimsuit.

"Are you coming in, Alika?"

I shook my head. "I was thinking. Maybe we should go home already? I've got extra credit to do for English."

"Can't it wait? Just for an hour? It's so hot today. And the water is so cool."

"She's right about that. Come on in, big

guy. I'll help you with your homework later."

I shook my head and sat down on a rock to wait for them. "Some other time, okay? You two go ahead."

While they splashed about, I stared at the heap of bloody white feathers and shivered.

I wanted to swim so bad, but I didn't dare, no matter how hot it got.

Someone had to stay out of the water.

Someone had to warn Jams and Uncle Paka if the shadow appeared.

Me and Jams had the eight to midnight watch that night. We were supposed to take over from Randy and Travis.

After supper, we told Mom and Kawika we were going over to Ku'ulei and Junior's for a sleepover.

Carrying our sleeping bags, flashlights and stuff, we left the house.

But instead of going over to the Fosters', we hid our sleeping bags in the garage.

Then we jumped on our bikes and pedaled downhill, to the valley.

I'd been right about the storm. It started raining big fat drops as we hiked up the valley to the *koa* tree.

The flashlight's narrow beam seemed so small in all that darkness.

Luckily, we knew the way blindfolded.

"Did you see anything?" I asked Randy and Travis after we climbed up into the tree house.

"Nah. Nothing." Travis yawned. "Come on, brah. Let's go home. See you, 'Lika. 'Bye, Jams."

"Laters, you guys."

Wind and rain rocked the tree as we sat there. It felt really weird when the tree house swayed. In the dark, it felt as if we were floating in mid-air, like a satellite drifting through space.

Jams was just getting sleepy when I heard the conch shell wailing. This time there were two mournful blasts.

I jerked my head around and stared at the ocean.

I was just in time to see the figure rise up from the glittering black water. It crossed the beach, then the road, then came up the valley, toward us.

"There! Do you see him?" I whispered as moonlight shimmered on a pale arm, then gleamed on a darker leg. "He's back!"

"I see him," Jams whispered shakily. "Where's he going?"

"To the falls. Come on! Let's follow him."

We climbed down the tree as quickly as we could. At least I did. Jams was slower.

"Alika? Let's go home. I'm scared," she whispered when we reached the bottom. "It's so dark and spooky here."

Her face was pale in the shadows. Her hair fell in wet rat-tails around her face.

I was soaked to the skin, and almost as scared as she was. But I was angry, too. Angry that people were coming into our valley. I was pretty sure they wouldn't be coming here at night unless they were doing something wrong.

"Don't be scared," I told her. "I'll be right beside you."

Grabbing her hand, I led her after me through wet ferns and dripping bushes.

Had the man we were following killed the cowbird, I wondered? Or had it been a hunter, like Don said? Or the black dog I thought I'd seen?

The moon stayed hidden behind a cloud until we reached the falls. When it raced free, it turned the falling rain into roaring sheets of silver all around us.

Lightning flashed. Its jagged bolts slashed the dark sky with bright arrows of light. Moments later, the thunder crackled so loudly, it made us both jump.

We crouched down behind some bushes. From there, we had a clear view of the roaring falls and the glittering black pool below it.

As the lightning flashed again, we saw a man standing on the rocks that surrounded it.

Jams looked at me. Her mouth opened in amazement. Her eyes were round. "But Alika, it's . . . !"

I looked at Jams and nodded. "Yeah, I know!"

We just couldn't believe our eyes.

It was . . .

CHAPTER SEVEN

. . . *Uncle Paka!*

"What's he doing here?" Jams whispered. "At night?"

"Shhh. Listen up. He's yelling something."

"*Aliiiiika! Jaaaaameee!*"

His voice carried faintly over the crackle of thunder and the roar of the rain.

"He's looking for us!" Jams whispered. "They must have found out we weren't at Ku'ulei's. He's not the one. We have to tell him we're here."

Before I could stop her, she stood up and ran toward him. "Uncle Paka! Here we are!"

She ran straight into his arms. He lifted her up and hugged her. "Jamie. Thank God, I found you guys! Your mom and Kawika are worried sick. Where's Alika? What are you two doing here?"

"We were going to ask you the same question, Uncle," I said, stepping out from my hiding place. "We followed you up from the beach."

Rain streamed down the lenses of his glasses as he nodded. "The beach was the first place I looked for you. Then I found your bikes down by the road and came up here. I thought you were at the tree house. But I couldn't find it in the dark."

"How did you know we weren't at Ku'ulei's house?" I asked.

He grinned. "You forgot your toothbrushes, Einstein. Your Mom decided to bring them over for you. Mrs. Foster told her there was no sleepover tonight. She made Junior tell her where you really were."

Great. We'd blown our cover because of a couple of stupid toothbrushes. Some Indiana Jones I'd turned out to be.

I made a face. "Exactly how mad is Mom?"

"On a scale of one to ten?"

I nodded.

"About a twelve point seven."

"And Kawika?"

"Whoa, big *pilikia*. Fifteen, maybe sixteen?"

"Oh, no."

"Oh, yes. When I left, he was imagining flash floods. Drowned step-kids. Broken legs, arms *and* necks. The works! He really cares about you guys, you know."

"Yeah. We know." I groaned. We were getting

to like him, too. Even if he wasn't our real dad.

"We'll be grounded till Thanksgiving, at least. Probably longer," Jams said.

"I guess we should go home now, then," I said with a sigh.

"I think so," Uncle Paka agreed sternly. "And the sooner the better. You're both soaked. And I'd say your mother's been worried long enough."

I couldn't sleep that night. I tossed and turned for hours.

Something was bugging me. It wasn't the chewing out we'd gotten from Mom. It wasn't the extra chores Kawika gave us as punishment, either.

It was way past midnight when I realized what it was. I couldn't believe I hadn't thought of it sooner.

If Uncle Paka had been looking for us, who had been blowing the conch shell at the falls?

Who—and *why?*

CHAPTER EIGHT

Me and the guys decided to shoot baskets after school on Monday. Randy and Junior were the Skins. Me and Travis were the Shirts. We played two-on-two until it got dark.

Ku'ulei and Jams made up the third team. Nā Wāhine, they called themselves. They wanted to challenge the winners from our game.

While they waited, they pretended to be cheerleaders. They used my Mom's new mop heads instead of pom-poms and shook them as they jumped up and down.

"W-Ā-H-I-N-E! YEEE—AAAY, NĀ WĀHINE!!"

The girls talked Randy and Travis into cheerleading next. They decided to use the mops as wigs.

Randy has a freckled baby face. He looked like Little Orphan Annie in the mop. Travis looked like his twin sister, Little Orphan Ugly. They looked so funny, doing jumping jacks and stuff, I thought I'd die laughing!

Go! Go! Go, team, goooooo!" they squealed.

"Okay, you guys. 'Nuff already. Are we playing ball, or what?" I asked, when we were all done laughing. "It'll be dark soon."

Bad mistake. When we started playing again, my team got its *'ōkole* well and truly kicked!

The Skins were twelve points up when I had to call a time-out. It was weird. I hardly had the ball all game, but I was gulping air and breathing hard.

Was I getting asthma, like Junior? His parents had put a pool in their back yard, so he could swim every day. Mrs. Foster told my Mom that swimming helped to open up his lungs.

Was that why I wanted to swim all the time? Because it was easier to breathe in the water?

"Hey. Time out, you guys. Our turn to be Skins now." I drank some water, then peeled off my tee-shirt.

"Whoa! Look at Alika's scar," Junior said. He stopped bouncing the ball to point at my back.

"Quit staring," I warned him, giving him stink-eye.

The other guys stopped dribbling the ball around. They stared at my scar, too.

"Wow. How come it turned black like that?"

Travis asked.

I shrugged. Why couldn't he just let it go? "Beats me," I said. "It's no big deal. Forget it."

"It's swollen, Alika. Jamie, look at this. Your brother should go to the hospital," Ku'ulei said, sounding bossy.

"For what?" I scowled. "It doesn't hurt."

"Alika's changing. That's what's happening." Junior said in that geeky way he has.

"Oh, yeah? You mean, like Superman?" Ku'ulei giggled. She covered her mouth with her hand. Her glossy black ponytail bobbed about, caught up in a bright green scrunchie.

"Not Superman, stupid." Junior made a gross face at her.

"What's he changing into, then? One vampire? One werewolf?" She made a goofy face at her younger brother and flashed me a grin.

It was my turn to stare at her now. She looked kind of cute in her lime-green top and denim shorts. I liked the way she took my side. I liked the way her mouth looked when she smiled, too.

Weird. I'd never noticed that before.

"Stupid yourself," Junior said. His eyes were round and dreamy as an owl's behind the thick lenses of his glasses as he added, "He's changing into . . . an alien."

The others howled with laughter. "An *alien?*"

"Yeah, right! I'm straight from Mars." I lifted up my hair. "Hey. Look under here, you guys. I've got eyes in the back of my head. Blaggh! Blaggh!"

I pulled my shirt back on. I'd had enough of them eyeballing my scar. No way I would admit that it worried me, too. "Now, cut it out, you guys. The only thing I'm changing into is . . . this tee-shirt. Da da!"

They laughed again.

"So, quit trying to throw off my game, eh? *Play ball!*"

We were still out there, shooting baskets, when the phone rang.

While the others went home to eat, I went inside to answer it.

It was Mom. She and Kawika were stuck at a meeting in town. They'd be home late, so they wanted Uncle Paka to take me and Jams out for dinner.

"Let's ride down to the valley," I told Jams when I went back outside. "We'll meet Uncle there. The valley's closer to Hale'iwa, so it'll be faster that way. I don't know about you, but I'm *starving*."

"Good idea. We can put our bikes in the station wagon," she said.

I nodded. "And maybe—just maybe—Uncle will take us to . . . Pizza Bob's?"

"Pizza Bob's! *Yes!*" Jams yelled. She gave me a high five. Her brown eyes sparkled. "Awesome!"

My sister loves pizza more than anything. I used to love it, too, with lots of extra cheese, olives, pepperoni and stuff.

But lately, all I wanted to eat was meat.

Lots of meat.

Our station wagon was still parked at the bottom of the valley beside Don's car. They must be working late at the dig.

We hiked up the narrow trail to the falls. The tree branches met over our heads. The leafy tunnel they formed was dark green and gloomy.

In fact, in places, it was so dark we had to feel our way, pushing between the bushes, scrambling over rocks and muddy ditches.

The air was so still and humid. It smelled of decay, damp leaves and wet earth. The swampy smells were suffocating. They made me feel like gagging.

I tugged at the neck of my tee-shirt, trying to stretch it. I wanted to make it looser. Maybe I'd grown since we went back-to-school shopping in September? Whatever. My clothes were choking me.

Jams had to slap her arms and legs every so often as we followed the trail to the falls. I could hear her muttering, "Oww! Ouch! Get away!"

All around us, mosquitoes hummed and whined. I could hear them. They sounded like fighter planes, but they never bit me anymore.

I don't know why, but they hadn't bothered me for the last couple of months. Maybe it was because my skin had grown so thick? The moskies couldn't bite through it.

When we were still several yards from the falls, we heard Uncle Paka's voice. He sounded as if he was arguing with someone, but who? Was it Don, or someone else?

It was hard to tell from there. Both voices were loud and angry.

"What's going on?" Jams wondered aloud. She started to go look.

"Hold on," I told her, holding her back by the arm. "Let's see who it is first."

CHAPTER NINE

"What were you trying to do with that conch shell?" I heard Uncle Paka yell. "Who were you calling?"

"Who do you think? *The Shark-Man!*" the second man answered.

It was Don's voice, all right, but it didn't sound much like him. His voice had changed. He sounded angry and kind of strange.

"The Shark-Man is only a myth, Don. An ancient legend. It's not real."

"No? Are you sure about that?" Don hissed. "What about the petroglyphs? How do you explain those?"

"The petroglyphs were your doing. You made them."

"No," Don said angrily. "That's where you're wrong, Paka. I found them. That's all I did."

"No. I don't think so. You see, I know the Association fired you last month. They called yesterday."

"So? My being fired doesn't change anything."

"I think it does. I think you made up the story about the Shark-God *heiau*. I also think you faked the petroglyphs."

"What! Why would I do that?"

"Because you thought the Association would rehire you if you had an exciting new find. But all you have is a great big fake."

"It's not a fake. Paka. Why won't you believe me!" Don said. "Back in the late 1700s, a shark-man attacked hundreds of swimmers in Kāmalū Bay and killed them. The people who lived here, in this valley, used spears and flaming torches to drive the monster from the bay, into a lava tube. Then they rolled huge boulders over both entrances to keep the shark-man imprisoned forever."

My heart started to thud with excitement. I'd seen lava tubes on the Big Island. They formed when an air bubble in molten lava cooled, forming a long cave or a tube, like a tunnel.

"What lava tube?" Uncle Paka asked. "Where?"

"The one that extends from this very pool down to Kāmalū Bay. The earthquake last August shifted the rocks that blocked its openings. *The*

Shark-Man is free to hunt again!"

Uncle Paka snorted. "Come on, Don. You don't really believe that?"

"Believe it? I've seen the monster with my own eyes!" Don hissed. "It walks on land. It swims in the ocean. It hunts wherever it wants, any time it wants!"

"Okay. So how does the conch shell fit in?"

"I've been using it to summon the monster each evening. I've been feeding it raw meat from the supermarket. It's the only way," he added ominously.

"The only way to what?"

"To control it. To keep it from attacking innocent people."

"Now I've heard everything. You really are crazy!" Paka exclaimed. *"Pupule.* A mental case!"

"No, Paka," Don said. He sounded very angry now. "I am something you have forgotten how to be. I am Hawaiian. I thought you would understand and help me. I prayed that together, we could drive the Shark-Man back into the lava tube. That we could keep the creature from hurting innocent people. Prevent it from making others into man-eaters. But no. You laugh at the

59

ancient beliefs of our people. You make fun of the old legends and call me crazy."

"You need help, Don." Uncle Paka's voice was gentle now. "Let me take you to a doctor."

"*A'ole!* No! If you won't help me, I must do it alone!"

"Wait. Don! Come back here!"

"Let go of me!"

From our hiding place, we heard a thud, then a grunt of pain, followed by a loud "splash!"

As the breeze blew in our direction, I sniffed. *Blood!*

A shiver ran through me. My mouth watered.

"Someone's been hurt," I told Jams. "Stay here. I have to find out if Uncle Paka's okay."

"I'm coming with you," Jams said firmly.

She was pale, but she looked like Mom when she made up her mind to do something.

Hard-headed and stubborn.

I sighed. "Jams, I . . . "

"I took First Aid at Girl Scouts, remember?" she cut me off. "Maybe I can help."

"Come on, then," I said.

We ran toward the falls.

When we got there, Uncle Paka was hauling

himself out of the falls. His clothes and hair were soaked. His nose was bleeding. His glasses lay on the grass, where they had fallen off. Luckily, they weren't broken.

There was no sign of Don.

"Sit down, Uncle Paka," Jamie told him. "Your nose is bleeding."

"Di dow it dis." He slumped down onto a rock. "Don dit me."

"Don hit you?"

"Des. Is it bwoken?"

"I don't think so," Jamie said. She pinched his nostrils together, right where his glasses had left a red mark.

She knew what she was doing. Almost at once, the blood stopped dripping.

I glanced down at the dark water and frowned.

As we ran toward the falls, I could have sworn I saw something move in its gleaming depths. Something that quickly vanished as Uncle Paka lifted himself out of the water.

"The earthquake last August moved the rocks that blocked its opening," Don had said.

A shiver ran down my spine. My hair crawled as it stood on end.

The shadow might have been my imagination. But I didn't think so.

"*The Shark-Man is free to hunt again!*" he'd said.

Could Don have been telling the truth?

"What happened?" I asked.

"It was Don. We argued. I tried to keep him here, but he punched my nose and ran off."

"How come?"

Paka sighed. "He was mad because I found out what he's been up to. He's in serious trouble with the Association, you see?" Uncle Paka said.

He squeezed the water out of his clothes as he talked.

"Why? What did he do wrong?" Jams asked.

"He lied, honey. He faked some petroglyphs several months ago, then pretended to 'discover' them."

"Why would he do that?"

"I think he hoped I'd be called back from Egypt to investigate his new discoveries. He wanted me to ask the Archaeology Association to re-hire him as my assistant, you see? I think he hoped his new 'find' would help him get his old job back."

"Then the petroglyphs are fakes?" I asked.

I touched the stone that hung around my neck. I was pretty certain *my* petroglyph wasn't a fake, even if the others were.

"I believe so, big guy. The Association director sent them to a lab on the Mainland to be dated. We should get the results any day now."

"But the *heiau* is real, isn't it?"

Uncle Paka nodded. "Oh, yes. It's an old fishing shrine, from what I can tell. Don has a different explanation for it, though. He thinks it's a shrine to the shark-god, or shark-man."

"What?" Jams laughed.

"That's right, honey. He claims a man-eating monster was driven into a lava tube between the falls and what you call Kapu Bay. It was trapped there by the families of its victims for hundreds of years, until an earthquake last August set it free."

"Wow! That's way cool!" Jams looked at me. Her golden-brown eyes sparkled with excitement. "Did you hear that, Alika?"

I nodded. "I heard."

August?

"That's some story," I said, frowning.

I'd just realized something. The end of August

was when I'd found my lucky stone in the bay.

The same month the huge shark had brushed against me.

The same month I'd got the dark scar that just kept . . . growing.

Was it a coincidence—or something else?

Paka pressed his lips together. "Don claims he's been feeding the Shark-Man raw meat each evening, to keep it from eating people." He shook his head. "The man needs serious help. He's imagining things now!"

We got Uncle's glasses for him. Then we all walked back down the valley to the car.

It was completely dark when we reached the station wagon. Don's car was gone.

Uncle Paka had some dry shorts and a tee-shirt in the back seat. After he'd changed, we stowed our bikes in the back and drove into Hale'iwa to eat dinner.

Less than a half-hour later, we were stuffing ourselves with a deluxe pizza at Pizza Bob's, playing the arcade machines and having a fun time.

"Hmm, this pizza is sooo good," Jams said. She took a huge bite and pulled back. Strings of mozzarella cheese stretched like elastic from the pizza wedge to her mouth.

Me and Uncle Paka laughed as Jams rolled her eyes and chewed. "Hmmmm. It's *'ono!*"

"In the morning, I'll call the Association and tell them what Don's been up to," Uncle Paka said. "They'll make sure he stays away from the valley from now on."

"Good idea," Jams said.

"Now. Let's forget all about him and just have fun. Okay, you guys? Alika, how about another pitcher of root beer to celebrate?"

"Celebrate what?" I asked.

He grinned and nudged Jams with his elbow. "What else? Never seeing Don again."

He was right about that.

Oh, man, was he ever.

CHAPTER TEN

A storm woke me up that night, after I'd gone to bed.

I opened my eyes. The room was so dark, the furniture made lumpy black shadows. When I was one small kid, it had looked like huge monsters, if I scrunched up my eyes. I was way past that now, I told myself.

Uncle Paka had left my closet door half open. Through the crack, I could see the glowing red eyes I'd stuck on my soccer ball.

They *were* just glow-in-the-dark stick-on ones, weren't they?

The wind whistled and moaned in the cracks and corners of our old house. It rattled the windows and shook the palm-tree fronds, so that they creaked and rapped against the windows like bony knuckles.

I swallowed nervously. The noises sounded like a wild animal, clawing and scratching to get inside.

To get at us!

Rain pattered across the roof like tiny gremlin feet, or dashed against the glass in angry bursts and sprays. It sounded as if someone was throwing handfuls of uncooked rice at my windows.

Suddenly, there was a thud against the wall across the room. I jumped about six inches—back under the covers.

In the bright lightning flashes that lit the room, I saw the curtains flying about.

Oh, great. The window had blown open. Rain was swirling inside, soaking the floor and Uncle Paka's bed. Why couldn't our old house have jalousie windows, like everyone else's?

"Uncle Paka?" I whispered. "Close the window."

His bed was across the room, right beneath it.

He must have been getting soaked, but he didn't answer, except for a loud snore. The lumpy shape of his body didn't move an inch, either.

"Uncle Paka," I hissed a little louder. "Hey. Wake up, Uncle! The rain's coming in."

He rolled over and made a snuffling sound, like Randy and Travis's dog.

In the end, I had to crawl out of bed and go close the window myself.

As I passed the clock radio on my nightstand,

I checked the time. It was past midnight.

I'd been asleep for over three hours, but I didn't feel rested. In fact, my whole body ached.

From across the street, I could hear Hoku, the Higas' Rottweiler, howling like a wolf. She was probably afraid of the thunder.

As I turned away, her howls got louder and more frantic. Then there was a loud "OOOWWW!" and the howling suddenly stopped.

Just like that . . .

"OOOWWWW!"

. . . then silence.

A wet, swishy gurgling sound replaced the hush.

Then something thrashed around in the shadows.

Something way big.

I pulled the curtains aside to get a better look. But even with my nose pressed up against the glass, I couldn't see what it was, or what was going on. It was too dark and the rain was too heavy.

I shivered.

To be honest, I was *glad* I couldn't see.

And then, just when I was going to dive back

under the covers, I saw a dark figure.

It ducked out of the shadows by the Higas' doghouse, then dragged itself slowly across the street.

Toward our house.

It was swaying from side to side as it came.

When it reached our back door, I lost sight of it.

Oh, no!

My hair stood on end. Chicken skin made pimples down my arms.

Whatever it was—whoever it was—could be in our carport right now, stealing our cars! Worse, it might be breaking into our house.

I swallowed. I had a scared, queasy feeling in my 'ōpū. Why had Hoku howled like that? What would have made a huge black Rottweiler stop howling, all of a sudden?

Grabbing my Louisville Slugger from the closet, I left my room. Uncle Paka was sleeping like the dead. No sense wasting my time trying to wake him up.

I'd wake up Mom and Kawika, instead, and tell them someone was trying to break in. They'd call 911. They'd know what to do until the cops came.

I knocked on their bedroom door.

No answer.

"Mom? Kawika?" I called softly.

Nothing.

Slowly, I turned the doorknob and went in.

CHAPTER ELEVEN

It was standing beside my mom and my step-dad's bed, and it smelled like rotten fish.

Looking down at them with its dead fishy eyes, it smiled a terrible, hungry grin.

I swallowed, trembling all over.

It was the Shark-Man, and it was over ten feet tall!

"Mom!" I croaked out. *"Wake up!"*

I'd never been so terrified in my life.

But each time I tried to scream Mom's name, nothing would come out.

Not even a squeak.

Just when I needed it most, I'd lost my voice. I couldn't even warn them.

In another second, that shark-thing would eat them alive!

And it would all be my fault.

Because I'd let them down.

Because I hadn't been able to stop it.

"Mom! Kawika! Wake uuuup!" I shrieked again and again as the monster bent over them.

Desperate, I flung my Slugger at the monster as hard as I could.

Big deal. It didn't even turn to look at me.

I grabbed Mom's high-heeled shoes from the closet and threw them at its head, one after the other.

The shoes bounced off its thick gray skin like raindrops.

I heaved Kawika's bowling ball over my shoulder and hefted it across the room next.

It slammed into the monster's head like a cannonball, then thudded to the ground and rolled away.

The Shark-Man didn't even blink.

Mom and Kawika didn't blink, either. They'd worked late the day before, and they were out for the count.

I was frantic, looking around for something else to throw, when the monster smelled me.

As it swung clumsily around to face me, its jaws parted.

"RRRRRRAAAAAGGH!" it roared.

My eyes bugging out of my head with fright, I stared into its huge, open jaws. It was like looking into a yawning crimson cave, with a fence of razor-sharp teeth.

Beyond the teeth, a dark throat fell away like a bottomless pit.

The cavern of doom.

"Moooom!" I croaked finally.

"Hmmm. Alika boy? Is that you, honey?" Mom asked.

Yawning, she leaned up on one elbow and rubbed sleepy eyes.

"Bad dream, sweetie?" she asked, squinting at the monster. "Alika, honey, you look terrible."

Oh, no. Mom wasn't wearing her contact lenses. She didn't know she was looking at the Shark-Man, instead of me.

"RAAAAAGGHH!"

The Shark-Man roared with pain as I slammed a heavy lamp at its nose.

That got its attention.

Turning, it lumbered away from Mom and came toward me. As it walked, it swayed from side to side like Frankenstein's monster.

Sure, it was swift and deadly in the ocean. But on land, the Shark-Man was as slow and clumsy as a fish out of water.

Its huge gray head was the flattened head of a shark. Its silver-ringed red eyes were cruel. Its smile was horrible.

Every inch of it was a merciless predator. A carnivore. A cannibal. A killing machine that ate raw flesh and blood.

Any flesh. Any blood.

And it was headed my way!

I ducked behind Mom's dresser, then launched myself through the open bedroom door, before it could turn around.

Like my hero, Troy Kahalewai, Puakea High's star linebacker, I dived down the hallway, headfirst.

"Yooowwch!" The carpet runner burned my face and hands as I skidded face down across the rug, but I didn't care. All that mattered was getting away, getting help, getting . . .

Oh, no!

Jams was awake. She was standing in the hall outside her bedroom door in her pink nightshirt. She must have seen the monster, because she looked frozen by fear.

"Run, Jamie. Runnnnnn!" I screamed. "It's coming!"

"I can't run. I'm too scared to m-move," she whispered.

I believed it.

Her face was white with terror. She didn't even blink as the hideous monster swayed down the hallway toward us.

"Go away! Leave us alone!" she yelled, trying to be brave.

But she didn't fool me. Even from down the hall, I could see her trembling.

I had to do something, but what?

The petroglyph stone.

The idea popped into my head like magic. The stone had protected me. Would it protect Jams, as well?

It had to. She wouldn't get a second chance.

The monster was smiling its terrible grin as it loomed over my little sister.

Its gloating smirk made my blood boil. I wanted to wipe that smile right off its face.

Tearing off my good-luck stone, I threw the cord over Jams's head and yelled, "Ruuuunn!"

When the monster saw the petroglyph, it roared with rage. Baffled, it turned away as Jams dived back into her room and slammed the door behind her.

Its massive, toothy jaws were wide open, ready to attack its next victim.

ME!

Chapter Twelve

I woke up in my own bed half an hour later. My head felt as if someone had kicked it. There was an ice pack under it.

Mom was sitting beside me. Her glasses were perched on her nose and she looked worried.

"What happened?" I asked. The last thing I remembered was a shower of white stars. They had exploded like fireworks in my head, just like in the cartoons.

"You fell down the stairs, big guy," Uncle Paka told me. He was standing at the bottom of my bed, next to Kawika. He tweaked my toes. "Bad dreams again, huh? What was it this time? Another mummy?"

"It wasn't a dream," I told him excitedly. "It was the Shark-Man. Don is right, Uncle. It's *real*. I saw it in Mom's room. When I tried to run away, I tripped and fell down the stairs and—oh, no!" I whispered. "Where's Jams? Did it get her?"

Frantic, I looked around for her, but she wasn't there.

"Calm down, honey. Jams is fine. She's

asleep in her room," Mom said, patting my shoulder. "Don't try to move, okay, sweetie? You have a big bump on your head."

"This is all Don Honu's fault," Kawika said. He scowled.

Usually, my step-dad is laid back and easy-going, although he's over six feet tall and lifts weights. But he looked mad now. Mad, mean, and real, *real* big.

"Those crazy stories of his! He better not come around here again, scaring my kids, giving them nightmares."

His kids? I blinked. I'd never heard Kawika call us *his* kids before. I didn't know that he worried about me and Jams, either.

But he did.

It was a pretty neat feeling. Somehow, it made up for not hearing from Dad since he went off to the Mainland with his second wife.

All of a sudden, I really wanted my step-dad to believe me. It was important, somehow.

"It isn't a story, Kawika. *Honest.* Mom, Uncle Paka, you *have* to believe me! Don was telling the truth," I told them.

I sat up in bed, even though my head ached so bad I felt like throwing up. I pushed the ice pack away.

"The legends are real. The Shark-Man was over at the Higas last night. In the morning, ask Mrs. Higa what happened to their dog, Mom. *Ask her!* I heard Hoku howling, and then . . . "

"Then what?"

"She just . . . stopped."

I swallowed. I remembered the gooshy, wet sounds and the thrashing noises I'd heard and I shuddered.

"I'll ask her. I promise, okay? For now, go on back to sleep, Alika, honey," Mom said. She used the voice grown-ups use when they want you to calm down, but don't really mean what they say.

In the end, I gave up and we all went back to bed.

The storm had died down, but the rain was still falling heavily outside.

Uncle Paka fell back to sleep as soon as his head hit the pillow. I waited until he was snoring, then got up and jammed my desk chair under the door knob.

I hoped Jams had done the same.

I wasn't taking any chances.

Maybe my family didn't believe the Shark-

Man existed. But I knew better.

I'd seen it.

It's funny what daylight can do. At night, in the dark, anything seems possible. Monsters. Vampires. Zombies. Werewolves. Shark-Men. It doesn't matter how crazy or wild these creatures might be during the day. At night, we believe they exist.

But by the time I was done eating breakfast the next morning, I was starting to think maybe Uncle Paka and Mom were right.

Maybe it really had been a nightmare. Maybe I'd imagined the Shark-Man trying to gobble up Jams. She didn't remember any of it—or so she said.

She was still wearing my lucky stone, though. Didn't that prove it had really happened? That the Shark-Man had been in our house?

"Are you *pau*, Alika?" Mom asked.

I was sitting at the table. Mom had the frying pan in one hand and a spatula in the other. Jams was chasing Cheerios around her bowl with a spoon.

"Some more scrambled eggs? How about a little more Portuguese sausage? Another scoop rice?"

I shook my head. "No, thanks, Mom. I'm all *pau*."

"Are you sure you're okay? You look a little gray this morning. That sleepwalking last night, I hope . . . "

"I'm fine, Mom. I'm going over to Randy's, okay?"

I couldn't wait. I had to know if Hoku was all right. If the dog was gone, then it meant I was right.

The Shark-Man was real.

"Now? What about school?" Mom asked.

She works as a greeter at Honolulu International Airport. That's where she met Kawika. He's a ticketing agent for the biggest airline.

She looked pretty in her purple-and-white flowered *mu'umu'u*. The white orchids in her hair were from the orchid plants she grew on our lanai.

"Are you going?"

"Of course I'm going."

"Well, the schoolbus will be here soon. Don't miss it. I can't drive you kids to school today, okay? I'm running late as it is."

I slung my backpack over my shoulder. "Don't worry. I'm ready. Tell Jams I'll meet her on the bus."

I didn't have to knock on the Higas' door to ask about Hoku.

Randy and Travis were going up and down the street, carrying an empty dog collar and a leash. They were looking in everyone's yard and calling their dog's name.

"What's up?" I asked. I felt sick inside. So sick, my stomach actually hurt. I had a feeling I knew exactly what was up. But I had to ask, anyway.

"It's Hoku. She ran away last night," Randy said.

He loved that dog. He looked upset about losing her.

"Mom said she was afraid of the thunder," Travis explained. "Dad said she ran off because she was scared."

I made a face. "That's too bad."

I had a pretty good idea what their dog had

been afraid of.

It wasn't thunder.

"Alika, will you help us look for her?"

"Sure," I promised unhappily. "I'll—er—I'll go ask the Fosters if they've seen her."

I wanted to tell them the truth. I *really* did. But how do you tell your best friends that a Shark-Man gobbled up their Rottweiler?

There was no sense in telling them. They'd never believe me, anyway.

Junior and Kuʻulei were in back of their house, staring at the pool.

"Have you guys seen Hoku?" I asked them.

"Randy's dumb dog? I didn't see her, but I heard her. The alien got her," Junior said in a Count Dracula sort of voice.

He was a real pain in the neck. "What alien?"

"The one that was swimming in our pool last night. Right, Kuʻulei?"

"Yeah, right," Kuʻulei said, rolling her eyes at me. Hands in her jeans pocket, she glared at her younger brother.

I glared at him, too. He didn't look as if he was lying, though. He'd seen something. But what?

My heart skipped a beat.

Could it be the same thing I'd seen?

Could his "alien" be my Shark-Man?

An icy chill snaked down my spine.

"You actually saw it?" I asked.

"Better than just saw. I took a picture with my new Polaroid camera. The one I got for my birthday."

A picture. Oh, man. He had a picture!

He looked to left and right. "That friend of your uncle's. He's one of them," he whispered, like a spy passing secrets.

"'One of them' what?" I whispered back.

"An alien. What else?"

"You think Don's an alien?"

"Yeah." Junior nodded. "I told you, I saw him last night. From my window. He blew on a conch shell, and then he dived into our pool. When he climbed back out, he'd changed."

"You mean he changed clothes, and *then* he got into the pool, *lōlō*," Ku'ulei corrected him.

"Unh-uh. I'm telling you, he *changed*. Into an alien. A creature that's half human, half sea-monster. It needs to go back into the water to breathe sometimes, or it'll die."

I was so stunned, I couldn't believe it. "You know what, Junior? You're *pupule*. Nuts!"

"Oh, yeah? What about this picture, then? How do you explain this?"

Chubby brown face beaming, he held up a blurred Polaroid snapshot. It was a picture of Don, all right. He was standing on the edge of the Foster's pool and he was staring at something. His mouth and eyes were wide open, as if he was screaming.

He looked terrified.

The picture must not have developed properly, though, because Don looked dark all over.

Or had he been standing in the *shadow* of something big.

I looked a little closer.

Oh, man. A shadow shaped like someone carrying a surfboard fell across Don's face.

Was it the shadow of the Shark-Man, as it came toward him?

Was that why he'd looked so terrified? Had he fallen into the pool, trying to lure the creature back to the valley?

"That's not an alien! It's just a snapshot of Don," I told Junior. "So what? This picture only proves he was trespassing on your property. It doesn't mean he's an alien."

"Wait. There's more," Junior said. "I found these at the bottom of the pool this morning, along with this." He held up Don's beat-up Nikes and a conch shell. "And this was in the carport this morning, after your friend left here in his alien form."

Junior held up a long, slimy black strand of seaweed. He pushed his glasses onto his nose. "There. How do you explain that, Alika?"

"Beats me. I don't know where it came from," I said, and shrugged. "Who knows? Maybe your dad went fishing last night? Maybe he dropped the *limu* in your carport. Did you ask him?"

"It wasn't in *my* carport, Alika. *Yours*. I found the seaweed in yours. After the alien went inside your house."

A shiver ran down my spine.

CHAPTER THIRTEEN

I thought about what had happened all that day at school, and in the weeks that followed.

But whichever way I looked at it, I kept coming back to the same answer.

The Higas' dog, Hoku, had vanished that night. So had Don Honu.

Junior had seen him go into the pool—but he'd only seen the Shark-Man come out.

Don hadn't changed into the monster.

Oh, no.

He'd become its victim.

I couldn't help wondering what he'd been doing in the Fosters' pool that night. Had he followed the Shark-Man to our street from the valley? Did he bring the conch shell to lead it away from us, with the promise of fresh meat? Had he risked his own life to save ours?

I think so.

But no one will ever know what really happened.

December came. We had a really great Christmas that year.

Uncle Paka was still staying with us, working on the fishing *heiau* for the Hawaiian Archaeology Association.

Dad and Aunt Joyce sent cards and presents from the Mainland. Mom and Kawika gave me and Jams a computer.

When the spring came, we still hadn't seen Don or Hoku since November.

Paka had reported his disappearance to the police, but no one found him.

I knew in my heart that they never would.

The weather was getting warmer now. The rainy season was over. We started making plans for a family picnic at the bay. It would be the very first picnic of the year.

Mom invited our friends along. We were really looking forward to swimming, diving and belly-boarding now that the rainy months of winter were *pau.*

It was a *fantastic* day for the beach. A perfect day, I thought, as we all piled into the station wagon, laughing and kidding around.

We could see the ocean below us as Kawika drove down the winding road to Kāmalū Bay. It was a beautiful turquoise blue and very calm. There was hardly a cloud in the sky, and the air was really warm and sunny.

A black *'iwa*, or frigate bird, drifted on the air currents high above the ocean.

"Look at that *iwa's* huge wingspan!" Uncle Paka said. He pointed through the car window at the sky. "From the ground, it looks like a pterodactyl."

We all laughed, but Paka was right. It did.

"Have you found many dinosaur fossils, Mr. Makahanaloa?" geeky Junior asked him.

We all groaned. Once you got Uncle Paka talking about his digs, you couldn't get him to stop.

He was still talking when we drove into the small parking lot.

After Kawika had parked, all of us helped to carry the mats, towels, cooler and other picnic stuff to the picnic table on the grass.

Once everything had been unloaded, the others stripped off their shirts, ready to go in swimming.

I was about to follow them when Kawika called me back.

"Alika, can you light the hibachi and make

the barbecue fire for us? I'm not too good at making fires."

"Sure," I said, grinning. Ever since Boy Scouts, I'd been pretty good at lighting fires. I was pleased he'd asked me. "Where's the charcoal?"

"Right over there."

I got to work, stacking the *kiawe* briquettes just right, adding the firelighter where it would do the most good.

Kawika and I were getting pretty tight. He'd been teaching me how to use the new computer to surf the net. He'd promised to take me fishing and scuba diving, too. I liked being around him, doing stuff together.

One day, maybe he could help me with my problem. But I wasn't ready to talk about it just yet.

I hung around for a while to make sure the charcoal was burning properly.

Uncle Paka and Kawika kidded around, laughing and arguing about who was the best cook and who was going to barbecue.

Paka won, but only because Kawika let him.

Pretty soon, the coals were really hot, a glowing orange color. The smell of burning *kiawe* filled the air.

"How do you want your steak cooked, Alika?" Uncle Paka asked. He was crouched behind the hibachi, holding a big metal pan of meat.

Smoke rose from the hot coals as he held up a pair of stainless steel tongs.

Dangling from them was a huge steak that dripped blood.

My mouth watered. Saliva gushed into my mouth.

"Rare, please," I told him, grinning. I licked my lips. "*Very* rare. Raw, in fact."

"Raw?" My uncle chuckled. "One tough guy, eh? Did you hear that, Lani? Your boy's a cannibal. A real man-eater."

"Raw! Eeeew. He's gross," Jams said, wrinkling her nose up at my steak. "That's what he is."

"It's Alika's steak, honey," Uncle Paka reminded her. "He can have it any way he wants it. Tell me how you want yours."

Jams made a face at me. "Well done, please. No blood in mine. *I'm* not a cannibal."

I bared my teeth at her and roared.

Kawika laughed. "You two. You're always

squabbling. Just like a pair of myna birds!" He ruffled Jams's hair and winked at me.

"Tell me about it," Mom agreed.

She was still smiling as she lifted a pot of rice onto the green picnic table. She took the rice scoop, some paper plates and chopsticks from the cooler.

"Alika. If you hurry, you have time for a quick swim before lunch. If not, you'll have to wait an hour after we eat. I don't want you getting cramps."

A swim before lunch?

Great idea. It would give me an appetite.

"Thanks, Mom. Laters!" I yelled.

I ran down the beach to the ocean. peeling off my tee-shirt as I went.

The scar on my back was swollen. Huge. I could feel it standing up, like a *kualā*. A fin.

A triangular dorsal fin.

Warm blue water surrounded me as I turned onto my side.

The smells of salt, *limu* and fish filled my nostrils as I swam out to the reef.

So did the scent of something else.

The delicious scent of fresh, warm blood.

Joy exploded through me.

I was here at last.

Here, where I belonged.

Here, where I could breathe.

With a powerful kick, I swam out to join my friends.

There was Randy, his dark head bobbing between the whitecaps. Beside him swam Travis.

Off to one side, Ku'ulei and her brother were dog-paddling about, treading water. Junior was whining that he'd cut his foot on some coral. Ku'ulei was scolding him.

It was Junior's blood I'd smelled.

"SHAARRKK!" he shrieked suddenly. His chubby brown face turned gray. "SHAAAAAAARRRKK!"

"SHAARRKKK!" Randy screamed, too. His eyes and mouth were wide with terror.

All of them started racing back toward the beach.

Their arms thrashed. Their legs kicked.

But I knew they'd never escape.

Not from me.

You see, the Shark-Man had chosen me to join him, months ago. That time in August, when he'd grazed my back, then let me go.

I was like him now. I had become a Shark-Man.

Human on land. Shark in the water.

I could go anywhere I chose.

Uncle Paka really should have listened to Don. He tried to warn him.

He really should have listened!

My black fin cut through the water like a knife as I streaked after them.

My jaws opened wide

. . . wider

. . . wider still!

My mouth watered.

There would be plenty of time for swimming later, I decided.

Right now, I was having friends for lunch.

Hmmm. *'Ono!*

Glossary

Aloha nui loa	warmest greetings, much love
Aloha ʻoe	farewell
ʻaʻole	no
bento	box lunch
grinds	slang for food
heiau	temple
ʻiwa	frigate bird
kapu	taboo; forbidden
kiawe	tree whose wood is used in cooking
kim chee	Korean pickled cabbage
kualā	dorsal fin
limu	seaweed
lōlō	crazy
make	die; dead
muʻumuʻu	loose dress
Nā Wāhine	The Women
ʻōkole	slang for buttocks
ʻono	delicious
ʻōpū	stomach
pau	finished
pīkake	small white sweet-smelling flower used in leis

pilikia	trouble
poi dog	mixed breed dog
poke	dish made with raw fish
pupule	crazy
sashimi	raw fish
stink-eye	dirty look
takuan	Japanese pickled turnip
ukus	head lice

About the Author

P.J. Neri is the author of twenty historical romance novels and four novellas for adults. Her books have appeared on national best-seller lists and received many awards. Her books in the Hawai'i Chillers series are her first titles for young people.

Born in England, P.J. has lived in Hawai'i for twenty-six years. She and her husband, Harvey, make their home in central O'ahu with four turtles and a dog named Heidi. P.J. and Harvey have three grown children, all of whom graduated from the Kamehameha Schools.

LOCAL KIDS LITERATURE SERIES

Angel of Rainbow Gulch
$6.95

Nēnē Award Nominee
Ka Palapala Poʻokela Award
Nominee

Secret of Petroglyph Cave
$6.95

Angel and Tūtū
$6.95

THE BESS PRESS